Sesame Street Start-to-Read Books™
help young children take a giant step into reading.
The stories have been skillfully written, designed,
and illustrated to provide funny, satisfying
reading experiences for the child just starting out.
Let Big Bird, Bert and Ernie, Oscar the Grouch,
and all the Sesame Street Muppets get your child
into reading early with these wonderful stories!

On *Sesame Street,*
Susan is played by Loretta Long
and Gordon by Roscoe Orman.

Copyright © 1988 Children's Television Workshop. Sesame Street MUPPETS © Muppets, Inc. 1988. All rights reserved under International and Pan-American Copyright Conventions. ® Sesame Street and the Sesame Street sign are trademarks and service marks of the Children's Television Workshop. Published in the United States by Random House, Inc., New York, and simultaneously in Canada by Random House of Canada Limited, Toronto, in conjunction with the Children's Television Workshop.

Library of Congress Cataloging-in-Publication Data:
Hautzig, Deborah. It's easy! / by Deborah Hautzig ; illustrated by Joe Mathieu ; featuring Jim Henson's Sesame Street Muppets. p. cm. — (A Sesame Street start-to-read book) SUMMARY: Big Bird regrets his decision not to let any of his friends help him plant his sunflower seeds when a flock of birds tries to eat his flowers. ISBN: 0-394-81376-6 (trade); 0-394-91376-0 (lib. bdg.) [1. Sharing—Fiction. 2. Gardening—Fiction. 3. Puppets—Fiction.] I. Mathieu, Joe, ill. II. Children's Television Workshop. III. Title. IV. Series: Sesame Street start-to-read books. PZ7.H2888Isb 1988 [E]—dc19 88-6441

Manufactured in the United States of America   1 2 3 4 5 6 7 8 9 0

A Sesame Street Start-to-Read Book™

IT'S EASY!

by Deborah Hautzig • illustrated by Joe Mathieu

Featuring Jim Henson's Sesame Street Muppets

Random House / Children's Television Workshop

Big Bird skipped down Sesame Street.
He had a shovel, a rake,
and a big bag of seeds.
"Big Bird!" said Ernie.
"Where are you going?"

"I am going to plant
a sunflower garden!"
said Big Bird.
"Gordon said I can use
his empty lot.
I love sunflower seeds!
I will plant them and
I will grow them...
all by myself!"

First Big Bird cleaned up the lot.
He gave the bottles, cans,
and other junk to Oscar.

Then Big Bird started to dig.
Grover came by on his bike.
"I, Grover the Planter,
am here to help you!"
Big Bird said, "I don't need help.
It's easy!"

Big Bird dug.

And Big Bird planted.

He dug and planted row after row.

The sun was very hot.

So was Big Bird.

Betty Lou came by with
a big cool drink for Big Bird.
He had planted all the seeds.
"Whew! Now I can go home!"
he said.

"No you can't," said Betty Lou.
"You have to water the seeds.
 They get thirsty too!"
 Big Bird groaned. He was so tired!
"I can help," said Betty Lou.
"I don't need help," he said.
"I can do it myself.
 It's easy."

Big Bird got a can of water
from Gordon's house.
"Oh, dear," he soon said.
"One little can of water
  is not enough for a big garden!"

So he went for water again…

and again and again.
At last he was finished
watering the seeds.

Big Bird was so, so tired.
He fell asleep.
He dreamed of rows and rows
of big yellow sunflowers.
"Wake up!" said Gordon.
Big Bird rubbed his eyes.
"Did my flowers grow yet?'
Gordon smiled. "Not yet, Big Bird.
Come on, I'll take you home."

The next morning Big Bird ran
to see his garden.
Susan came to visit.
"Why do you look so sad?" she asked.
"My flowers didn't grow!" he said.
"It takes time," said Susan.
"Your flowers will start to grow
in a week or two. You'll see!"

Every day Big Bird went to look.
He looked very, very closely.

And finally his plants
did start to grow.

Soon the flowers were
as tall as Grover!
One day they started to droop.
Big Bird was very worried.
"My flowers are sick," he said.
"I will ask Dr. Keats what to do."

Big Bird went to the doctor's office.

He told Dr. Keats

all about his flowers.

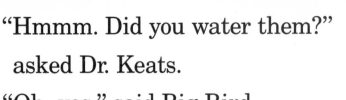

"Hmmm. Did you water them?"
asked Dr. Keats.

"Oh, yes," said Big Bird.

"As soon as I planted them!"

Dr. Keats said, "You have to
water them again.

Flowers get thirsty."

So Big Bird ran to his garden
and watered his flowers.
Dr. Keats was right!
All the flowers stopped drooping.

All summer long
Big Bird's flowers grew.
They grew as tall as Big Bird.
Grover and Ernie and Bert
liked to sit in the shade
under the biggest flowers.

One day Gordon said, "Your flowers
will soon be ready to pick.
I will be glad to help you."
But Big Bird said, "No thanks.
I will pick them myself.
It's easy."

At last the flowers were ready.
Big Bird was ready to cut them.
But suddenly he heard flapping.
Lots of flapping. He looked around.
Birds were everywhere.
Sparrows, blue jays, pigeons—
all kinds of birds.
"Oh, no!" cried Big Bird.
"Those birds are eating
my sunflower seeds!"

"Go away! Shoo! Scat!"
yelled Big Bird.
But the birds kept coming,
and the birds kept eating.
"This is terrible!" he cried.
He ran up and down the rows.
He yelled at the birds.
He shook his rake at them.
Grover came running.
"Big Bird, what is wrong?" he asked.
"HELP!" cried Big Bird.
"Help, help, help!"

Everyone on Sesame Street
came to help.
Even Oscar came.
He banged on his lid and yelled,
"GO AWAY! GO AWAY!"
Together they all chased the birds.

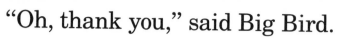

"Oh, thank you," said Big Bird.
"You rescued my flowers!"
"We were happy to help!"
said Grover.
"Now we can help pick them.
Okay, Big Bird?" asked Gordon.
"Oh, yes," said Big Bird.
"I can sure use some help!"

At last the sunflowers were picked.

Big Bird had bags and bags of seeds.

"Oh, my. There are SO many seeds!

Please, everybody take a bag!

I can never eat all of them!" he said.

"Thank you, Big Bird," said Susan.

"Next year we can all plant things

and share the work."

"That's a great idea," said Big Bird.

And he really meant it!